The Star of the Zoo

Virginie Zurcher

Daniel Howarth

QED Publishing

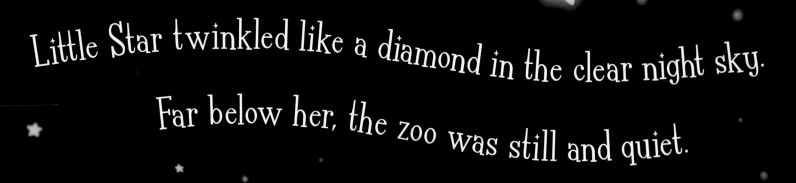

Little Star twinkled like a diamond in the clear night sky.
Far below her, the zoo was still and quiet.

This book belongs to:

....

....

For Arno and Penelope, the sparkling stars
in my heart - Virginie Zurcher

For Ben, I know you'll reach the stars
one day! - Daniel Howarth

Editor: Ruth Symons
Designer: Anna Lubecka
Editorial Director: Victoria Garrard
Art Director: Laura Roberts-Jensen

Copyright © QED Publishing 2014

First published in the UK in 2014 by QED Publishing
A Quarto Group company, The Old Brewery, 6 Blundell Street, London N7 9BH

www.qed-publishing.co.uk

A catalogue record for this book is available from the British Library.

ISBN 978 1 78171 659 5

Printed in China

The animals were getting ready for bed.

Then suddenly...

Little
Star
lost
her
balance
and
tumbled
out
of the
sky!

Down,
down,
down
she
fell,
like a
shooting
star.

She left a sparkling trail all the way to the ground.

"Ouch!" she cried
as she landed with
a bump.

All the animals ran to
see what had happened.

"Oh no! Are you alright,
Little Star?" asked Zebra.
"Can we help you?"

"I need to get back into the
sky so I can twinkle like
a diamond," Little Star
said sadly.

"I'll help you," said Lion. "I'm the strongest animal in the zoo."

Lion picked up Little Star, climbed onto a rock, and lifted her high into the air.

Lion could lift Little Star
easily, but he couldn't
reach the sky.

"I can help!"
called Ant.

"Rahahaha," laughed
Lion, "you're too small.
You can't help."

"I'll help you," said Monkey. "I'm the best climber in the zoo."

Monkey picked up Little Star and jumped into a tree. He swung through the branches to the very top.

Monkey climbed as high as he could, but he couldn't reach the sky.

"I have a plan!" called Ant.

"Hoohoohaha," laughed Monkey, "you're too small. You can't help."

"I'll help you," said Giraffe.
"I'm the tallest animal
in the zoo."

Giraffe picked up Little
Star, stood up straight,
and stretched her neck
as far as she could.

Giraffe was very tall, but she couldn't reach the sky.

"I know what to do!" called Ant.

"Heeheehee," laughed Giraffe, "you're too small. You can't help."

Little Star's
brightness
was fading.

"I have to be back in
the sky before sunrise,"
she cried.

"Give me a chance - I can help!" called Ant.

The animals all just stared at Ant. What could she do?

"Well, if you think you can do it, you might as well try," said Lion, rolling his eyes.

Ant scuttled off...

She came back, not with ten, not with a hundred, but with thousands of friends to help.

Ant picked up Little Star, and climbed onto another ant's back.

That ant climbed onto another ant.

And that ant climbed onto another.

The
tower
of
ants
grew
higher
and
higher
until...

...they reached the sky!

"You did it!"
shouted Little Star.

All the animals cheered.

"Anything's possible
if you work together!"
Ant said proudly.

Next steps

Show the children the cover and look at the book's title. Ask the children where they think the story takes place.

Ask the children if they have ever been to a zoo. What was their favourite part of the zoo and why? Do the children know where the animals in this book would live in the wild?

While reading the story, did the children predict what would happen next? Did they think that Ant would be able to help?

Discuss what it feels like to be the youngest or the smallest in a group or a class.

How did Ant and her friends help Little Star? Ask the children if they think the other animals learned anything from this. Discuss the importance of teamwork. Can the children think of a time when they achieved something with the help of their friends?

Think about the book's title. Who is the real star of the zoo? Can the children think of another good title for the story?

Ask the children to draw their favourite part of the book or their favourite zoo animal.

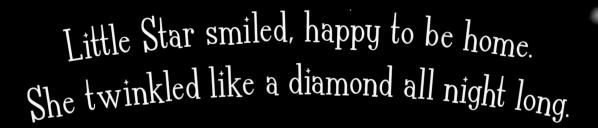

Little Star smiled, happy to be home.
She twinkled like a diamond all night long.

Far below, the animals finally
snuggled down and went to sleep.